the 329th friend

the 329th friend

by Marjorie Weinman Sharmat
illustrations by Cyndy Szekeres

Four Winds Press   New York

Library of Congress Cataloging in Publication Data

Sharmat, Marjorie Weinman.
   The 329th friend.

   SUMMARY: Bored with his own company, Emery Raccoon invites
328 guests to lunch but finds that none of them have time to listen
to him.
   [1. Friendship — Fiction. 2. Animals — Fiction] I. Szekeres,
Cyndy. II. Title.
PZ7.S5299Tk   [E]   78-21770
ISBN 0-590-07558-6

Published by Four Winds Press
A division of Scholastic Magazines, Inc., New York, N.Y.
Text copyright © 1979 by Marjorie Weinman Sharmat
Illustrations copyright © 1979 by Cyndy Szekeres
All rights reserved
Printed in the United States of America
Library of Congress Catalog Card Number: 78-21770
1 2 3 4 5 83 82 81 80 79

For Barbara

Emery Raccoon woke up,
dragged himself out of bed,
and made a face.
"Another day with Emery Raccoon," he said.
"Who needs it!"
Emery looked in the mirror.
"Blah! The thought of
spending another day with myself
makes me want to
go back to bed!"

Emery went to his kitchen
and ate a dish of cold mashed potatoes.
"There is only one thing more boring
than cold mashed potatoes.
Me!"

Emery looked out the window.
"Maybe there is somebody out there
who will think I'm more fun
than cold mashed potatoes," he said.
"Maybe there is somebody out there
who will come over here
and be my friend."

Emery got dressed and went out.

"I'll invite somebody over," he said.

"Or a couple of somebodies.

Maybe three would be nice.

Four might be even better.

Five would be almost as good as six."

Emery thought for a while.

Then he invited 328 guests to lunch.

"Three hundred and twenty-eight new friends
and rotten old me," he said.

Then Emery peeled 329 potatoes,
picked 329 bunches of vegetables,
cracked and cooked 329 eggs,
and baked 329 tarts.
"I hope nobody wants seconds," he thought.

Emery went to his yard
and set some tables.
"I'm glad I own a lot of tables, dishes,
and glasses. And silverware," he said,
as he set 329 spoons, 329 forks, and 329 knives.
"And now for the napkins.
I don't have napkins.

Oh, well," said Emery,
as he cut up one dozen bedsheets
into neat little squares.

After he'd picked 329 bouquets of flowers
and put them in 329 vases
on the tables,
Emery heard a loud noise.
"My new friends are coming!" he said.
"It sounds like an army.
A big friendly army."

Emery's guests arrived one by one
and in pairs, threes, fours, fives,
tens, twenties, and fifties.
"Hello, Possum," said Emery.
"Hello, Squirrel," said Emery.
"Hello, Bear, Bear, and Baby Bear. Hello, Spiders.
Hello, Toads. Hello, Porcupine and Porcupine.
Hello, Goose. Hello, Squirrel.

Hello. Hello. Hello. Hello. Hello. Hello. Hello. Hello.

Glad to see you," said Emery 328 times.

"Glad you could come."

"And come. And come. And come."

"And come."

Emery's guests swarmed over every inch of space.
And when they all talked at one time,
it sounded like a great roar.
"A great,
                friendly
                            roar,"
                                        thought Emery.

Emery's guests sat down to eat.

Crunch, munch, chew, bite, swallow, gulp.

"It certainly sounds different
than one raccoon eating mashed potatoes
all by himself," thought Emery.

Emery sat down at the head
of the longest table
and started to eat.

"Please pass the ketchup," he said.
But nobody answered him.
"Please pass the ketchup," said Emery
in a louder voice.

But still nobody answered him.

"KETCHUP!" yelled Emery.

Nobody paid any attention to him.

"Maybe eggs taste better
without ketchup," thought Emery,
as he looked down at his eggs.
Then he turned toward Owl
who was sitting to his right.
"Eggs taste better without ketchup,"
said Emery.
But Owl was talking to Mouse.
Emery turned to his left.

"Maybe it is easier to talk to everybody
than somebody," thought Emery.
"I will stand up
and everybody will notice."
"Have you ever eaten eggs
without ketchup?"
he asked Possum.
But Possum was busy munching and crunching.

Emery stood up.

"AHEM!" he said.

Nobody looked at Emery.

"EMERY RACCOON IS SPEAKING!"

yelled Emery.

But everyone

just kept on talking and eating and eating and talking.

Emery gnashed his teeth.

"I cooked! I set tables!

I picked flowers!

I cut up sheets!

I worked my paws to the bone.

But nobody talks to me.

Everyone has a friend here but me!"

Emery picked up his dishes, his glass,

his silverware, his napkin,

and his vase of flowers.

"Excuse me," he said to his 328 guests

even though he knew no one would listen to him.

Emery went inside
and spread a tablecloth
on the floor.
He took a bottle of ketchup
from his refrigerator
and put it on the tablecloth.
Then he carefully placed his dishes
and glass next to the ketchup.
He set his silverware in neat rows
beside his dishes.
He placed the vase of flowers
in the center of the tablecloth.
Then he turned on his record player
to soft music.
He tucked his napkin under his chin.
Then he picked up his fork and started to eat.

"Everything looks tasty, Emery," he said.

"Glad you think so, Emery.

Please pass the ketchup, Emery.

My pleasure, Emery.

Fine meal. You're a perfect host, Emery.

And you're a perfect guest, Emery.

Thank you, Emery."

Emery hummed to the music while he ate.
"I have a good hum," he said.
"I should hum more often."
He told himself a joke in his head
and he laughed.
"I should tell myself a joke
more often," he said.

He thought about interesting things
he hadn't thought about
in a long time.
He made up an exciting story
but he saved the ending for another day
to surprise himself.

When Emery finished eating,
he leaned back.
"I am full of something good
and it's more than lunch.
I am full of myself.
What a good friend I am.

I know what I'm thinking.
I know what I'm feeling.
I am quiet, but I hum nicely.
I even have fine table manners.
I am an exactly right friend.
How lucky I am
to have a friend such as me."

Suddenly Emery remembered his guests.

He ran outside, humming.

 **"EMERY!"** shouted his guests.

"My name is Bayard," said Owl.

"That's a nice hum you have.

 And your eggs taste fine without ketchup."

"Definitely," said Possum.

"I'm Rosalind and you set a great table."

"I agree," said Mouse. "Alonzo Mouse here.

 I was just asking, 'Where is our friend Emery?'"

"Well, as you see, your friend Emery Raccoon

 is right here," said Emery with a smile.

After lunch, each of Emery's 328 friends
said, "Thank you, Emery."
And some said,
"Please come to my house very soon."
"I will," said Emery.

Emery said good-bye to Bayard Owl,

Rosalind Possum,

Alonzo Mouse,

the Goat Twins, Zachary and Whackery,

Mrs. Elephant and her son Maurice,

Anastasia and Joe Toad,

the Barbara Spider Family, Irving Fox,

Marjorie and Mitchell Mouse,
the John Chipmunk Jug Band,
Miss Imogene Squirrel,
and all his other new friends.
"Have safe trips home," he said.

Then he got to work.

"Everybody used a main dish

and a dessert dish

and a glass," he said.

"That's three times 329

which is 987.

Everybody used a fork, knife and spoon.

That's another 987.

So I have 1,974 things to wash

and 329 squares of torn-up sheets to clean
and approximately 100,000 crumbs to sweep.
But it's worth it.

Today I found a good friend

I never noticed before.

Today Emery Raccoon found Emery Raccoon."

Emery washed and cleaned

and swept into the night.

When he was all finished,
Emery had some tea and toast
with his 329th friend,
and thought what good company he was.